WEIRD PARENTS

AUDREY WOOD

PUFFIN BOOKS

PUFFIN BOOKS
Published by the Penguin Group
Penguin Putnam Books for Young Readers, 345 Hudson Street,
New York, New York 10014, U.S.A.
Penguin Books Ltd, 80 Strand, London WC2R ORL, England
Penguin Books Australia Ltd, Ringwood, Victoria, Australia
Penguin Books Canada Ltd, 10 Alcorn Avenue, Toronto, Ontario, Canada M4V 3B2
Penguin Books (N.Z.) Ltd, 182-190 Wairau Road, Auckland 10, New Zealand
Penguin Books Ltd, Registered Offices: Harmondsworth, Middlesex, England

Originally published in hardcover by
Dial Books for Young Readers
A Division of Penguin Books USA Inc.

First Puffin Pied Piper Printing 1995
ISBN 0-14-054924-2
A Pied Piper Book is a registered trademark of Dial Books for
Young Readers, a division of Penguin Books USA Inc.,
® TM 1,163,686 and ® TM 1,054,312.
20 19 18 17 16 15 14 13 12 11

*The art for each picture was created using colored pencils,
watercolor wash, and pen and ink. It was then color-separated
and reproduced in full color.*

PARCHEESI is a registered trademark of Milton Bradley Company.

WEIRD PARENTS
is also available in hardcover from
Dial Books for Young Readers.

For Arthur Levine,
who has weird parents too.

There once was a boy who had
weird parents.
No matter how many times he told them not to,
the weird parents did weird things whenever
they went out into the world.

In the morning the weird mother always walked the boy to his bus stop.

"Bye-bye, honeycakes!" she'd call.

Then as the bus drove away, she'd blow a huge kiss
and press her hand to her heart.

At twelve o'clock when the boy opened his lunchbox, he'd always have a weird surprise.

And in the afternoon the weird father always walked him home. But not before he shook hands with everyone he met.

"Pleased to meet you. How do you do? Isn't it a lovely day?" he'd say.

More than anything, the boy dreaded the family's
night out on the town. Every Saturday evening

the weird father put on his weird hat and the weird
mother combed her hair in a weird way.

Then they would dance all the way down the stairs
to their weird car.

They were always early for the picture show, so the
boy had to stand in line with them.

The weird mother always talked about the boy as if he wasn't there.

"My son has a belly button that sticks out. No one else in our family has one like it."

And the weird father always asked the boy to do
something silly.

"Walk like a chicken," he'd say.

Of course the boy wouldn't, so the weird father did
it instead.

When the movie began, the boy tried to enjoy it,

but his weird parents always laughed out loud when
no one else did.

At least things got better after the movie. The weird
father always treated them to ice cream cones. And the
weird mother always let the boy pick out a comic book.

At home they all played a double round of Parcheesi.®
And the weird parents never got mad if the boy won
both games.

And when they tucked him into bed and kissed him good night, the weird parents always sang a little song.

> "Sweet dreams,
> We love you,
> Good night,
> Now don't let the bedbugs bite,
> Don't let the bedbugs bite."

But as the boy lay in bed trying to go to sleep, he couldn't

help wishing his parents weren't weird anymore.

Then he wished everyone else had weird parents.

Yet he knew that wasn't possible.

And somehow it didn't matter....

After all...

they were his parents, weird or not.